A GIRL, a BOY, and THREE ROBBERS

A GIRL, a BOY, and THREE ROBBERS

GAIL GAUTHIER

illustrated by JOE CEPEDA

G. P. PUTNAM'S SONS

G. P. PUTNAM'S SONS

A division of Penguin Young Readers Group. Published by The Penguin Group.

Penguin Group (USA) Inc., 375 Hudson Street, New York, NY 10014, U.S.A.

Penguin Group (Canada), 90 Eglinton Avenue East, Suite 700, Toronto, Ontario M4P 2Y3, Canada (a division of Pearson Penguin Canada Inc.). Penguin Books Ltd, 80 Strand, London WC2R ORL, England. Penguin Ireland, 25 St. Stephen's Green, Dublin 2, Ireland (a division of Penguin Books Ltd.). Penguin Group (Australia), 250 Camberwell Road, Camberwell, Victoria 3124, Australia (a division of Pearson Australia Group Pty Ltd). Penguin Books India Pvt Ltd, 11 Community Centre, Panchsheel Park, New Delhi - 110 017, India. Penguin Group (NZ), 67 Apollo Drive, Rosedale, North Shore 0632, New Zealand (a division of Pearson New Zealand Ltd). Penguin Books (South Africa) (Pty) Ltd, 24 Sturdee Avenue, Rosebank, Johannesburg 2196, South Africa. Penguin Books Ltd, Registered Offices: 80 Strand, London WC2R ORL, England.

Printed in the United States of America.

Design by Gina DiMassi and Marikka Tamura. Text set in Mendoza Roman.

Library of Congress Cataloging-in-Publication Data

Gauthier, Gail, 1953– A girl, a boy, and three robbers / Gail Gauthier ; illustrated by Joe Cepeda. p. cm. Summary: Three afternoons a week, Brandon reluctantly stays with his imaginative classmate, Hannah, and her oversized cat, Buttercup, playing games, but their adventures really begin when the dreaded Sunderland triplets from next door try to steal Buttercup. [1. Play—Fiction. 2. Imagination—Fiction. 3. Cats—Fiction. 4. Neighbors—Fiction.] I. Cepeda, Joe, ill. II. Title. PZ7.G23435Gl 2008 [Fic]—dc22 2007023967

ISBN 978-0-399-24690-6

1 3 5 7 9 10 8 6 4 2

For Bruce—thanks for the squirrel

Contents

Chapter 1

Vampires
in the
Hallway

Hannah Dufrane slid along the wall in her family's upstairs hallway. She was probably pretending she had trouble seeing, even though it wasn't all that dark. She'd closed all the bedroom doors so no sunlight could come in. She hadn't turned on the ceiling light, either. It was still bright enough in the hallway so that I didn't have any trouble seeing her skinny body coming toward me. Her little white face between her long, dark braids would be easy to see almost anywhere.

I was sure she had a reason for trying to make the hallway look dark. I just didn't know what it was. I didn't know why she was making me lie on my back on the hall floor, either. She hadn't bothered to tell me. I didn't ask because I like lying on the floor.

I did ask about the awful smell, though. I didn't like that.

"What stinks?" I said.

"You're not supposed to talk," she complained.

"Why not?"

"You're dead," Hannah explained.

"Darn it. How did that happen?"

"You were killed by a vampire."

"Okay!"

The awful smell got stronger. It was like a cloud over me. My eyes started to burn.

"Whad is dat?" I asked. The words didn't sound quite right because I was holding my nose.

"Garlic powder. Vampires hate garlic. They never suck the blood out of anyone who eats pizza."

"Ick! Get it away from me!" I yelled.

"Are you kidding? If you were killed by a vampire, then you're a vampire now, too. You're going to be hungry soon. I'm using this garlic powder to trap you in the hallway so you can't destroy everyone in the house."

I rolled over onto my stomach and tried to escape on my hands and knees.

"Why didn't you just hold a cross up in front of me?" I asked as I tried to get away. "On TV people always hold up crosses in front of vampires. Crosses shoot some kind of death rays at them. Especially silver crosses."

"Turn around," Hannah ordered.

I looked over my shoulder. Hannah was holding up a table knife and a fork that she had tied together with something. They looked a little more like an X than a cross, though.

I held my arms up over my head.

"Stop! Stop! It hurts!" I shouted as I rolled over on my back again.

We could hear someone running below us. Hannah's mother, Mrs. Dufrane, called up the stairs, "Hannah! Leave Brandon alone!"

"We're just playing vampire!" Hannah called back.

"Well, be careful." Then Mrs. D. went, "Oh, yuck. What are you doing with garlic powder? I can smell it all the way down here. You two are going to have to clean up that mess when you're done."

"It was all Hannah's idea!" I told her.

"Brandon, it's *always* Hannah's idea," Mrs. D. said.

That was true. I would have been very happy to watch TV on Monday, Wednesday, and Friday afternoons when I had to go to Hannah's house after school, because my mother worked. But oh, no. Hannah always had an *idea*.

Now she pulled one of those long cardboard tubes out from under her arm. She held it up over her head and brought the end of it down on my chest.

"Yeow!" I yelled as the tube bent under Hannah's weight. "What do you think you're doing?"

"I'm plunging a stake through your heart," she said. "You're toast."

"Game's over then, huh?"

"It didn't last very long," Hannah said sadly.

"That's okay. We can probably find something to watch on Animal Planet now."

I was getting up, trying to brush garlic powder off my clothes, when we heard scratching coming from behind one of the closed bedroom doors.

"What's that?" Hannah hissed.

"Sounds like—"

"Another vampire," Hannah whispered. "It's the old vampire that bit you and sucked your blood. He's coming to get revenge on the vampire hunter who destroyed his new creation."

"That means he wants revenge on you," I pointed out.

"Yes," Hannah said with a big smile.

"How come you always get to play the person the bad guys want to track down for revenge? I never get to be anything good."

"What are you complaining about? Being a vampire

is a good part. Now hold this," Hannah said, shoving the knife and fork cross at me.

"I can't. I'm a vampire. Crosses shoot death rays . . ."

"That's all over because you've been staked."

Sometimes I have trouble keeping up with Hannah.

"Now I need you to be my assistant," she continued.

"Oh, sure. I'm always whatever you *need* me to be. What about what I *want* to be?" I demanded.

Hannah sighed. "What do you want to be?"

I thought for a minute. "I don't know," I admitted.

"Take this," she said, shoving the cross at me again. "An evil vampire is waiting for us on the other side of this door. We've got to destroy him or he'll make more vampires. Then they'll make more vampires. And *they'll* make more vampires. Soon the whole world will be filled with vampires."

"I was a vampire for a while," I reminded her. "Just a few minutes ago. It wasn't so bad. Except for the garlic."

In fact, if it hadn't been for the garlic, I would have liked being a vampire. I've always wanted to be one. Nobody messes with vampires.

Hannah finally just stuck the cross in the top of her pants. Then she reached for the doorknob and wiggled it.

The scratching on the other side got louder.

"He smells fresh blood," Hannah explained.

She bent over and started searching for something on the floor. When she stood up, she had the bottle of garlic powder. She took the lid off. "We've got to be ready for anything."

Sure. No matter what happens, a person can take care of it with garlic powder.

Hannah turned the knob and slowly pushed the door open.

A big, fat, orange cat slipped through the opening. He was missing a part of one ear and the tip of his tail.

"Buttercup!" Hannah wailed, holding the garlic bottle out in front of her with both hands. "My Buttercup! *You* are the evil vampire who sucked the blood out of Brandon? I never knew! My heart is broken!"

"Yeah. Mine, too," I said as I grabbed the garlic powder away from her. "That cat stinks so bad sometimes that the smell of garlic would be an improvement. I'll give him a few shakes of this stuff."

But as soon as I tipped the bottle of garlic powder, Buttercup was off like a shot to the end of the hallway and then down the stairs. He was gone before the powder got anywhere near him.

"That vampire was too old and smart for us," Hannah said sadly. "He beat us. He'll probably go through the whole house, biting plants . . . slippers . . . my stuffed animals . . . and turning them into bloodsucking creatures of the night. We are doomed."

"Good. I'm going to go watch TV."

"I don't want to do that," Hannah said. "Let's think of something else to play."

"Well," I suggested, "we could pretend we were

going to a movie. The chairs in your family room could be the seats in the theater, and your TV could be the movie screen."

"That sounds boring," Hannah replied.

"Then how about playing space shuttle? The chairs in your family room could be the seats in the space shuttle," I explained, "and your TV could be a two-way camera back to Earth. We'd have to sit and look at it so we could talk with people."

Hannah groaned. "That doesn't sound very interesting."

"Yes, it does!"

Her eyes suddenly got really big, and she sort of smiled, which meant she was getting an idea.

"I know!" she exclaimed. "Let's play mummy! We'll get some towels and wrap you up tight so you can't move!"

Talk about a game that didn't sound very interesting.

"Okay," I agreed. "So long as my mummy coffin is the couch in front of the TV."

THE
TEA PARTY

Chapter 2

When we got to Hannah's house after school the next Monday, the coffee table in the family room was all set up for a tea party.

Boy, do I hate tea parties.

Whenever she has one, Hannah makes us eat off her tiny toy dishes. We can never get much food on the plates or much juice in the cups, so it takes forever to get enough to eat and drink. The food isn't all that good, either, because she makes it herself the night before. It's either dry or soggy from sitting around so long. All the plastic wrap Hannah uses doesn't help a bit.

And then there's the cat hair all over the coffee table

and the little dishes. (And everything else in Hannah's house.) I've eaten more than my share of cat hair at Hannah's tea parties.

When I saw the tea things, I dropped my backpack on the floor and said, "Oh, no. I am *not* pretending to be a prince who has asked you to tea because he wants to marry you. I told you I would never play that game again. And I'm not pretending you're some kind of fairy queen who is lost and has to drink special tea or she'll die. I'm tired of playing fairy games."

"This is a war game," Hannah explained as she brought the food from the kitchen.

"It's not some kind of fairy kingdom war game, is it?" I asked.

I love war games. But putting the war game in a fairy kingdom would ruin everything, because in fairy kingdoms anything can happen.

That sounds like a good thing, but it's not.

"No, it's an England war game," Hannah answered.

"Because there are lots of fairies in England, right?"
I was sure she was going to get around to fairies. I could just feel it.

"No, because in the game we live in London, a city in England. There's a big, big war going on, and London is bombed a lot. So our parents send us out to the country to live in a big house with a family. That way we'll be safe."

"I don't get it," I said. "If the war is somewhere else, and we're safe, how is this a war game?"

"We're in the big house in the country because of the war, so it's a war game. And our parents aren't here, so we can have adventures. Sit down, and I'll pour you some tea."

Hannah isn't very good at pouring tea. She always gets it all over the saucers and even onto the food. Since the tea she uses is really juice, that's not so bad. It does make everything sticky, though.

"Adventures? What kind of adventures?" I asked.

"That depends. We can live with a crabby old man

and woman who don't like kids but learn to love *us* because we're so nice," she suggested.

"That doesn't sound like much fun. Besides, I don't think it would ever happen. We're not that nice."

"I am," Hannah insisted.

"Not really. We need a different adventure."

"We can meet all kinds of strange neighbors," Hannah said.

"How strange?"

"Maybe some could be witches or enemy agents trying to destroy a bridge or something because of the war."

"That's good," I agreed. "We could fight with them." I love fighting with witches and enemy agents.

"I saved the best idea for last," Hannah said. She looked really pleased. "We could go into a closet that has a fake door in the back. When we go through the fake door, we'll be in a magic kingdom."

"A fairy kingdom, right? I knew it! I knew somehow you were going to work fairies into this thing."

"No, I wasn't thinking of fairies at all."

Uh-oh. "You were thinking of a magic kingdom where trees and bunnies talk, weren't you?"

"Sort of," Hannah admitted. "And everyone would sing. There would be lots of singing."

"Forget it. Let's do the strange neighbor adventure. Where are we going to find one? Your mother won't let us leave your yard."

"Buttercup can be our first strange neighbor. We'll invite him to tea."

"I don't think he likes juice," I said. "He might lick the butter off some of these sandwiches, though."

"We'll find some leftover meat in the fridge. If he's going to be a neighbor and we're going to invite him here, we should serve him something special."

As if he would notice. He eats plants.

The problem with Hannah's plan was that we didn't know where Buttercup was. He could be anywhere, doing anything. He was a lot like a fairy that way.

We hunted for him all over the house. We checked every piece of furniture he liked to sleep on or scratch.

We looked in all the bedrooms. Hannah tried to make me go into the big closet in the spare bedroom to see if he was there.

But I knew she was trying to trick me. Once she had me in a closet, she would have tried to get me to play that magic kingdom game with her. The next thing I knew, she'd be singing like Snow White and I'd be stuck playing one of the seven dwarfs or something. I wasn't falling for that.

So instead we went outside to hunt for our strange neighbor.

"Buttercup! Here, kitty, kitty, kitty!" Hannah called once we got outdoors.

I don't know why she bothers. That cat never comes. She'd have a better chance calling the red squirrels that make themselves at home everywhere on her street.

We hunted for Buttercup all over the yard. We checked the old, overgrown flower beds that Buttercup likes to use for litter boxes. We looked in the strip of trees that separated the Dufranes' yard from all the other yards beside and behind them. We climbed a big tree so we could look at all the neighbors' lawns from up high.

"We can also use this for a lookout post to watch for enemy aircraft," Hannah said once we were up there.

"You said the bombing was in London and that we were far away from there," I reminded her.

She shrugged. "Sometimes planes get lost."

"Yeah. Like your cat."

We couldn't see a cat in the yard to our left or the yard to our right. But the Coopers lived right behind the Dufranes, and from the house next to theirs we could hear something that sounded very suspicious.

THE STRANGE NEIGHBORS

Chapter 3

"Nice kitty. Nice, nice kitty."

Hannah turned and looked at me. "The Sunderland triplets have my cat!"

The Sunderlands aren't really triplets. They just look like they are. They're all nearly the same size because the bigger kids are twins and the younger one is really big. *Really* big. Like he's going to end up being a giant. Also, the girl has short blond hair and the boys don't get their blond hair cut anywhere near often enough. You can usually tell Rose from her brothers, though, because she's the scariest.

She's the scariest kid in the first grade. Her brother, Owen, is the second scariest kid in the first grade. Even the kids in Hannah's and my grade know that. Even our teachers know. The lunch ladies, the parents who come in to help with parties, the school bus drivers—everyone knows about them.

Someday their little brother is going to have to start school, too. Then there will be scary Sunderlands in two grades. I can't wait.

I didn't think the three of them had Hannah's cat, though.

"No one would call Buttercup 'nice kitty,'" I told her. "They must have another cat back there."

Then we heard Mrs. Sunderland shout, "Owen! Rose! Conor! Leave that nasty cat alone! It looks as if it has some kind of disease!"

"Now *that* sounds like Buttercup," I said.

We jumped down from the tree and headed over to the back corner of Hannah's yard that touched one of the back corners of the Sunderlands'.

From there we could see one blond kid trying to reach for Buttercup's tail while the other two shouted, "Get him! Get the cat!"

"Run, Buttercup! Run!" Hannah screamed.

When Hannah screams "Run," I start moving. She has a scream that would be perfect for some kind of monster on TV. In real life, though, you just want to get away from it.

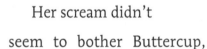

Her scream didn't seem to bother Buttercup, though. He just stood there with the Sunderland triplets surrounding him while he twitched his tail back and forth. Then he crouched down. His tail was still going.

He looked as if he had everything under control.

Hannah went charging through the trees onto the Sunderlands' property.

"Hannah! We're not supposed to leave your yard!" I yelled after her.

"I've got to save my cat!" she shouted back at me.

"He doesn't need saving!" I told her.

Then I thought, Hey, wait a minute. Whenever we're playing a game, Hannah or Buttercup almost always gets to save whoever needs saving. I hardly ever get a chance to do anything like that. If Buttercup really was in trouble, this might be my lucky day.

So I started running through the trees, too. "Don't worry, Buttercup!" I shouted. "I'm coming!"

One of the triplets looked up and saw us running toward them.

"Grab him, Owen!" Rose ordered. "They're going to try to steal our cat!"

Owen took a step toward Buttercup. Before he could even get close, Buttercup took off between the boy's legs. He headed into the woods and out of sight.

Rose said to us, "Look what you did. You made little Conor cry."

Both boys looked dry-eyed to me. Then one of them hit the other, who instantly started crying as if someone had turned on a faucet.

"What did you do that for?" I asked Owen.

"She told me to," he said, pointing at his sister.

"Did not," Rose said.

Conor was crying so hard, you'd have thought he needed an ambulance. The tears were pouring right out of him as he knelt down next to a hole in the ground. When he stood up, he was holding a clump of dirt in his hand. He threw it at me.

"Hand grenade!" Hannah shouted. "Dive! Dive!"

We both jumped out of the way, threw ourselves down on the ground, and covered our heads. The clump of dirt didn't make much noise when it hit the ground, so I went "Pow!" because it felt a little foolish to have dived out of the way of something that just went plop.

"That was a close one," Hannah said as she started to get to her feet. "Watch for land mines," she told me as I stood up.

The lawn looked as if it really was covered with land mines. Holes had been dug all over it. Some of them were filled with water or mud. A couple of short shovels were lying on the grass, and a watering can was turned on its side.

"How could this happen?" I asked. "The enemy was supposed to be bombing London."

"They've invaded here, where our army wasn't expecting them. We've got to warn headquarters," Hannah informed me.

I looked over at the Sunderland triplets. All three of them were staring at us with their mouths open. Conor stopped crying and started sucking a dirty thumb.

"Rose! Owen! You aren't talking to strangers, are you?" Mrs. Sunderland called from the house.

Rose turned toward the house and shouted, "They stole our cat, Mom. We had a cat, and they made it run away."

Conor started crying again. "Wanna cat!" he wailed. He started running from hole to hole, picking up clumps of dirt and throwing them at us. He slipped into one of the wet holes and fell. When he stood up, he had mud all over his legs and bottom.

He'd stopped crying, though.

"I told you not to play with that dirty stray cat!" Mrs. Sunderland called.

"Rose made me do it!" Owen yelled.

"No, I didn't!" Rose said.

Mrs. Sunderland came out onto the deck. She didn't seem bothered by all the holes in her lawn, but she did look surprised when she saw us.

"What's going on?" she asked.

"Strangers!" Rose shouted.

Then the boys started in, too. "Strangers!" they shouted while they ran around in circles. They stopped every once in a while to point at us.

Their mother yelled at them a few times to be quiet. That didn't do any good, so she finally stepped down off the deck and came over to us.

"I live over there," Hannah told her, pointing toward her house. "We just came over to get my cat. Who isn't dirty, by the way."

He is, but I didn't want to argue about it just then.

"My cat! My cat!" Conor shrieked.

"It came in our yard, so it was ours," Rose insisted.

"Everything that's in our yard is ours," Owen added.

Mrs. Sunderland sighed and looked as if she was going to fall down. Then she noticed the mud all over Conor's bottom half.

"Conor, what did you do to yourself?" she asked.

Conor looked down at himself and smiled. "Made poopy all over."

Rose and Owen laughed.

Mrs. Sunderland groaned. Then she looked at us. "They have to come in now," she said to us. "Maybe you can play with them another time, if you want."

"We're not allowed to leave Hannah's yard," I said quickly. I wanted to make sure she didn't think we were ever coming back. "Ever. Not ev—"

"That would be great," Hannah said, ruining everything.

No, it wouldn't, I thought. I was afraid someone

would start making plans for a playdate, and then what would I do? But Conor saved the day.

"No! No! No! Don't want to go in!" he shouted as he started to run toward a little shed at the back of the yard.

"Rose, Owen, help me catch your brother," Mrs. Sunderland begged. "If he locks himself in the toolshed, we'll never get him out."

"I'm not touching him," Rose said. "He's covered with poopy."

"Me neither," Owen agreed.

"He's not covered with poopy," Hannah told Mrs. Sunderland. "He just fell in a muddy hole. They're all just playing a game."

What kind of people play a game like that?

I don't know how long it took Mrs. Sunderland to catch Conor or if he locked himself in the toolshed. We left to go back to Hannah's, running from tree to tree in the woods between the backyards. Hannah said we had to be careful because we might be captured by pilots from downed enemy aircraft.

"We *are* going to have to be careful," I told her. "The Sunderland triplets know you live close to them now. You live *way* too close to them, Hannah."

"I really do have strange neighbors," Hannah said.

She sounded a lot happier about that than I was. The Sunderland triplets were definitely not the witches or enemy agents that I'd been hoping for.

Chapter 4

A SURPRISE

"Oh, Father! Father! My feet are gone! Make me new ones! Now!" Hannah said.

"Um . . . okay," I replied.

We were in Hannah's garage playing Pinocchio. She'd just finished reading the book and insisted it would make a great game. All I knew about Pinocchio was that he was a puppet that became a boy.

Like that would ever happen.

She got to be Pinocchio, of course, and I was stuck being the old guy who carved him out of wood. At least I got to pretend to use some of her dad's tools.

"Oh, Father! Father! Buy me things! Buy me a coat

and a hat! Buy me a spelling book so I can learn to read like a real boy," Hannah ordered.

"But you're a girl, Hannah," I pointed out.

"I'm a *puppet*, Brandon!"

"Then you're a *girl* puppet. If you become real, you're not going to become a boy."

This had to be one of Hannah's worst games ever.

Mrs. D. came into the garage from the kitchen. "I have a surprise for you guys," she said.

"Oh, good!" Hannah exclaimed. "We're going to Disney World, aren't we?"

"Not today," Mrs. D. told her.

"You found a genie in a bottle?"

Mrs. D. sighed and shook her head. "We're going to have some visitors—"

"From outer space?" Hannah broke in.

"No," Mrs. D. replied. "From the street behind ours. You know the Sunderlands?"

"Uh-oh," I said.

"Mrs. Sunderland just called. Her husband was supposed to come home early from work to watch the kids because she has to leave for an appointment. But he's going to be late, and she wanted to know if they could come over here until he comes to get them."

"Why did she ask you? The Sunderland triplets never come over here," I pointed out.

"Where's their mother going?" Hannah asked before Mrs. D. could answer me. "You think she's going to the doctor, and she'll have to go the hospital? Because then the Sunderland triplets will have to stay here for *weeks* or even *months*. They can all sleep in sleeping bags on the floor in my room. Or maybe she's going to visit the boarding school she's going to send her kids to and they'll have to eat watery soup for dinner every day, and Brandon and I can help them escape. Or maybe—"

Mrs. D. ignored Hannah and spoke to me. "Mrs. Sunderland called me, Brandon, because she said my daughter and her little boy friend had been over to her house a couple of days ago. She said that since you all know one another, anyway, having them come over here would be like a playdate for you."

"You told her I'm not Hannah's *boyfriend*, didn't you?" I said.

"I didn't think of that because I was so surprised to hear that the two of you had left the yard."

Mrs. D. didn't sound surprised when she said that. She sounded mad.

"We had to go, Mom," Hannah explained. "We were on a rescue mission. The Sunderland triplets had captured Buttercup, and we had to save him."

"I *knew* we shouldn't have gone over there," I said. "Buttercup never needs to be saved. Now we're stuck with the Sunderland triplets for nothing."

Just then someone started shouting in back of the house.

"No! No! No! Don't want to go!"

"That sounds like Conor. They must be on their way over," Hannah said. She looked at me and smiled. "This is going to be so much fun."

"No, it's not! We're—"

I stopped talking because I could see Mrs. Sunderland coming through the woods, and I didn't want to be rude or anything. Not that she could have heard me. She was carrying Conor, who was yelling his head off, and she was dragging Owen behind her while she kept shouting to Rose to hurry up.

Mrs. D. leaned down between Hannah and me and whispered, "See? When you leave the yard, bad things happen."

She didn't have to convince me. I felt as if I was in one of those TV shows where bad guys suddenly show up at your front door and start pushing their way into your house. There's just nothing you can do to keep them out. You're doomed.

As the Sunderlands got closer, I could see that Conor had his finger up his nose, which was probably why he'd finally shut up. Rose seemed to be scratching her backside. And Owen was trying to kick his sister while being pulled along behind his mom.

"They're so excited about coming here," Mrs. Sunderland gasped.

"No, we're not," Rose said.

I guessed Rose didn't worry about being rude the way I did.

Mrs. Sunderland handed Conor to Rose and whispered, "Hold on to him until I'm out of sight." Then she told Conor his sister would take care of him, and she ran back to her yard.

I don't think I've ever seen a mom move that fast.

Mrs. D. told us she'd be inside if we needed her. She disappeared into the house pretty quickly, too. Then Hannah and I were left alone with the Sunderland triplets.

"We're only staying until our father gets home," Rose announced after the grown-ups were gone. "Don't get any ideas about us eating dinner here or anything."

"Don't worry," I replied.

"You showed up at the perfect time," Hannah told her.

What was she talking about? There was no perfect time for them to show up.

"We're playing Pinocchio and need more people," Hannah explained.

Rose let go of Conor. She gave him a little shove so that he wasn't hanging on to her anymore.

"I hate Pinocchio," she said.

"So do I," Owen agreed. "What is it?"

"Pinocchio is a story about a puppet who is always having adventures," Hannah told them.

"That sounds stupid," Owen said.

"Stupid, stupid, stupid, stupid, stupid," Conor repeated as he ran circles around Rose.

Hannah looked at him. "Conor, you're going to play Pinocchio."

"What?" I shouted.

I *never* get to play the best part in any of Hannah's games. Now she was going to just hand one to one of the Sunderlands, who had never even been in her yard before?

"Conor is the smallest. He looks the most like a puppet," Hannah said.

"He's almost as big as Rose and Owen," I argued.

"But he *is* the smallest," Hannah said again. "If we try hard, we might be able to carry him like a puppet."

"No," Conor yelled. "No, no, no, no, no."

Then he started running.

"Catch him! Catch him!" Hannah screamed. "Pinocchio is escaping from the wood-carver's workshop!"

We all took off after Conor.

THE
PINOCCHIO
GAME

Chapter 5

Hannah told Owen he was the wood-carver who made Pinocchio, which had been my part. I didn't mind losing it because Hannah said the wood-carver had to go to prison in the garage. Owen didn't seem to have any problem with that. Especially when Hannah made the rest of us play other puppets who meet Pinocchio along some road.

"Pinocchio! Come get hugs from your wooden brothers!" she shouted to Conor.

"No, no, no," Conor yelled back while he kept running all over the backyard.

After we finally caught him, Rose said, "Now what?"

"Now I'm going to be a cricket that talks to Pinocchio," Hannah announced. "I am a Talking Cricket," she said to Conor, "and I am going to tell you something important."

What could a cricket have to say that was all that important?

"Boys who refuse to obey their parents will never be happy," Hannah said very seriously.

There was a moment of silence while we all looked at her.

"That's it?" I asked her.

"And if you keep behaving the way you're behaving, you're going to turn into a donkey and everyone will laugh at you," Hannah went on.

That was better.

"A cricket is just a bug, Conor," Rose told her brother. "Squish it. Squish the bug."

Conor laughed, raised his foot, and hopped toward Hannah.

Hannah threw herself against a tree and slid down it, clutching her chest. "You better watch it, Pinocchio," she moaned. "You're going to end up on the

Island of Toys, and you know what will happen there? You'll . . ."

But before Hannah could finish speaking, she made a choking noise, stuck her tongue out, closed her eyes, and slumped down on the ground.

"Oh, no, Pinocchio! You killed the cricket!" I said. "That can't be good."

"Does that mean this stupid game is over?" Rose asked.

"No," Hannah said as she jumped up. "Now Pinocchio has to do a whole bunch of bad stuff."

Rose smiled.

"Bite?" Conor suggested, sounding hopeful.

That would have been bad. But before Conor had a chance to give biting a shot, he was distracted by a blur of dark red that roared out of the woods and across the driveway.

"Cat!" Conor called, pointing.

He was wrong. The red thing wasn't a cat. The cat was the larger orange blur that ran across the yard next.

"Hey!" Owen shouted. "Something's trying to get me in here."

We found Owen standing on the hood of Mrs. D.'s car when we got to the garage. He pointed toward the tool bench next to the kitchen door. Under it, Buttercup had cornered something that was frantically running back and forth and chattering.

"It's just a squirrel," Hannah said.

"Let's catch it!" Rose exclaimed.

"Didn't anyone ever tell you to stay away from wild animals?" I asked.

"No." Owen grinned and took two steps toward the edge of the car hood. Each time his foot came down on the hood, the metal sank a little bit under his weight. Then when he moved his foot, the metal came back up, making a popping noise.

He was still up there when Mrs. D. opened the door from the kitchen and came out to see what was going on. He wasn't there when she went back inside. He was out in the yard with the rest of us. The squirrel had been chased outside with a broom and had gone up a tree. Buttercup was stretched out on the driveway.

"If your mother had let us stay in the garage, we

could have caught the squirrel in that cat carrier I found," Owen complained to Hannah. "It was the only good thing you have in there."

"What would you have done with the squirrel if you'd caught it?" I asked.

"Taught it tricks," Owen said.

"You can't teach squirrels to do tricks," I told him.

"I could have," Owen insisted.

"Let's teach the cat a trick," Rose said. "The cat's here at least."

"You can't teach Buttercup anything," I replied. "No one can."

"Buttercup doesn't have to learn anything. He's perfect the way he is," Hannah said.

Not really.

"Cat," Conor said, reaching for Buttercup. "Wanna cat."

"He was our cat for a little while," Rose reminded him. "Then he was stolen away."

Conor started to cry. It's creepy the way he can just do that with no warning at all.

"He wasn't *really* your cat," Hannah said. "You can't just kidnap things and say they're yours."

"Why not?" Rose asked. "Once we have something, it *is* ours."

That's what she thought. No one ever *had* Buttercup.

"Daddy," Conor said, pointing into his yard. A car was parked there, and a big blond man was getting out of it.

"We're going home. But first we need to finish this game," Rose announced. "This cat can be Pinocchio. He really is small enough to carry."

She bent down and lifted Buttercup into her arms. Then she looked around at all of us.

"And now," she said, "Pinocchio is going to run away." She turned and started running for her house.

"Run, Rose! Run!" Owen shouted as he raced after his sister.

Hannah was right behind them, shouting, "Give me my cat!"

"Never!" Rose yelled over her shoulder. "Once we're in my yard, he's mine."

I didn't get excited about helping Buttercup this time. I knew I didn't have a chance of saving him. He was Buttercup. He saved himself. But I thought I might have a chance to save someone else, even if it had to be Rose.

And I do love saving people. No matter who they are.

"Let him go, Rose!" I shouted as I ran past Conor and moved up in the line of kids running toward the Sunderlands' house. "He doesn't like people to run with him! He doesn't like to be jiggled. He's going to—"

Before I could say "scratch you," Rose suddenly stopped running and started to howl. At almost the same time, Buttercup leaped from her arms, hit the ground, and started running for home.

Rose stood in her yard looking down at her arms. They had long scratches running from her elbows to her wrists.

"What did you let him go for?" Owen demanded when he reached her.

"He scratched me!" Rose cried. And I mean she was really crying. "He cut me up."

Conor turned around and started back toward Hannah's yard. "Cat!" he called. "Cat!"

Hannah stepped in front of him and wouldn't let him pass.

Conor started to cry again, Rose was already crying, and Owen started shouting at both of them. Mr. Sunderland, who was still out by his car, just looked scared.

We stayed in the trees between the yards until after the Sunderland triplets had chased their father into their house.

Hannah turned to me and smiled. "That was a good game," she said.

I didn't think it was really *good*. But the Sunderlands did make the Pinocchio game a lot less boring.

THE MUSEUM OF CAT

Chapter 6

"What is this?" Mrs. D. asked us after school one day the next week. She had marched us right up to Hannah's room after we got off the bus. We didn't even get a chance to take off our backpacks or raincoats.

I knew what was coming long before we got to Hannah's bedroom and Mrs. D. pointed to the floor of the closet. I had told Hannah it wasn't a good idea.

But she never listens to me.

"Eww. What's that smell?" I asked.

We looked in the closet. Hannah had pulled all her shoes and toys off the floor and replaced them with a big shoe box lid filled with cat litter.

"Uh-oh," Hannah said.

It turns out that a shoe box lid is nowhere near big enough to use as a litter box. But Buttercup had tried. There was litter all over the floor, and what was left in the box just wasn't enough to do the job, which was why the closet smelled.

He had also chewed through the box of cat food Hannah had left for him. He got that all over the place, too. He hadn't opened his jug of water, though. That was good.

"Well?" Mrs. D. said.

"The closet is a giant safe for locking up treasure," Hannah explained.

"Why does it need a litter box?" Mrs. D. asked.

"Because Buttercup is the treasure."

Mrs. D. looked surprised. I guess Buttercup wasn't the first thing she thought of when she heard the word *treasure*.

"You see, our house is a museum, and Buttercup was a stuffed animal that people could come look at. But he came to life, and now he's worth a lot of money, so we need a safe to keep him in when the museum is closed."

Like anybody would go to a museum to see a cat—stuffed or alive.

"Hannah's the boring person who takes people around the museum and shows them things," I told Mrs. D., "and I'm the guard. Don't you think I should get to carry a gun? Just a pretend one? I can bring some from home. I've got a bunch."

"I know, Brandon. You've told me about your guns before," Mrs. D. said. "But I think most museum guards just carry two-way radios on their belts. No guns."

"Two-way radios, Brandon!" Hannah exclaimed. "My grandmother gave me some. I'll get them. Then while you're doing your guarding, I can give you orders. That will make the game so much better. "

I didn't really see how giving me orders could make anything better.

Mrs. D. laughed. Then she said, "No radios until you've cleaned up this mess, Hannah. And don't make Brandon do it. He's your guest."

"He almost lives here," Hannah complained.

"But not really," I said as I hurried out of the room.

I could hear Hannah running after me. "Make your rounds of the museum," she shouted from her doorway. "You have to check all the windows and doors, you know."

"Yeah, okay," I said as I ran down the stairs.

I decided I would use a computer monitor to check the doors and windows. Guards on TV did that all the time. So I went into the family room and turned on the television. It really did look like a computer monitor. If I had my way, we'd use it in our games all the time.

I stretched out on the sofa and changed channels with the remote until I found a cartoon about a teenager who led a small band of humans against the robots who had taken over his high school. Talk about a good show!

During a commercial, I switched to Animal Planet for a while. I don't usually get to watch television at Hannah's, so I didn't want to waste any time. When I changed back to the cartoon, the teenager was about to turn off the power supply that controlled the evil gym teacher. It was really exciting, so at first I didn't notice I wasn't alone anymore.

"What are you doing?" Hannah asked.

"I'm watching a monitor connected to cameras that cover the doors and windows of our museum," I replied.

"No, you're not. You're watching Cartoon Network!"

"Well, the monitor is connected to that, too," I admitted. "It's . . . a magic monitor!"

"Does your magic monitor tell you where Buttercup is?" Hannah asked. "He *is* the most valuable thing in the museum. You need to know where he is all the time."

"Let me see," I said. I started flipping through channels. "Oops. It looks as if he's missing."

"How could this happen? What kind of guard are you?"

"I'm a pretend guard, Hannah."

Hannah rolled her eyes, handed me a radio, and

told me to turn it on. Then she ran out of the room.

But after the radio in my hand made a buzzing noise, her voice came out of it, giving me orders just as if she were standing in front of me.

"Go upstairs and hunt for Buttercup."

I pushed the button that would let me talk back to Hannah. "But I can check all the rooms right here from my computer monitor."

"Turn off the TV, Brandon!"

I didn't need the radio to hear that. I turned off the TV and slowly went upstairs.

"What are we looking for?" I asked into the radio once I'd checked all the bedrooms.

"Buttercup! Haven't you been paying attention?"

"He's not here," I told her.

"Then look for clues."

"How will I know I've found one?" I asked.

The radio buzzed and then Hannah's voice said, "Look for blood. Bullet holes in the walls. Broken windows. Ransom notes."

It would be so cool to find any of those things.

I checked the window in Hannah's room. It wasn't broken. I buzzed Hannah on the radio.

"I think I found a clue," I told her.

"What? What?"

I said, "Well, I can see Buttercup through the window. He's outdoors on the lawn."

"Is he hurt? Does he look as if he just escaped from robbers?"

"No, he's chasing squirrels."

"Squirrels!" Hannah repeated. "How many of them are out there?"

I had to take a guess. "A bunch."

"A gang! Buttercup has been stolen by a gang of art thieves!"

TRACKING THE THIEVES

Chapter 7

By the time we got outside, the gang of art thieves was gone. This was about what I'd expect of squirrels. They don't hang around long. They're not like cats. I don't think I've ever seen a squirrel taking a nap in the yard.

"Where could they have taken him?" Hannah asked.

I didn't remind her that the squirrels weren't taking Buttercup anywhere. He was chasing them. She would have just told me that I was ruining the game.

"Squirrels have nests in trees," I said. "Way up."

We looked up toward the tops of the trees that surrounded Hannah's backyard. That was pretty much a waste of time because it was May, and you can only see squirrels' nests in the fall and winter when there are no leaves on the trees. We could see lots of squirrels running around up there, though. They looked as if they might be playing tag.

"Maybe they'll send a ransom note," Hannah suggested.

"What do you think they'll want?" I asked. "Nuts?"

"Lots of them," she replied. "Poor Buttercup. He must be so scared."

I had to laugh. Buttercup is never scared. He scares everyone else.

"We'd better try to track them. Maybe we can catch them before they drag him up to their hideout in a nest. You start over on the other side of the house and look for squirrel footprints," Hannah ordered.

Squirrel footprints? I thought we had a better chance of finding Buttercup giving himself a bath than we did of finding squirrel footprints. But I went over to the part of the yard I'd been told to search and started looking. I still had my radio and kept reporting back to Hannah on my progress.

"Nothing so far . . . nothing by the lilac bush . . . Hey, I found the mitten I lost last winter. It's all stiff on the outside, but it's really heavy. Wait. I think there's something living in—"

The radio in my hand made a buzzing noise, and Hannah's voice came out of it. "Stop talking," she whispered. "And come over here."

"Be right there," I called into the radio.

I found Hannah in the corner of her yard nearest the Sunderlands' house. She was watching the Sunderland triplets drag a piece of paneling from their garage over to a tree. They propped it up and started throwing things at it.

Hannah nodded at them. "Target practice," she said in a low voice. "I bet they're working with the art thieves."

I didn't think the Sunderland triplets could work with anyone. But I liked the idea of target practice.

"Oh, we should do that, too," I told her. "You never know when you'll need to throw something."

"It looks boring," she complained. "What's the point?"

"You throw something at a board and hit it. What do you mean, what's the point?"

"And what are they throwing?" Hannah asked. "It doesn't sound like rocks."

Just then, we saw Owen and Rose start fighting over something in a yellow can.

Hannah answered her own question. "They're throwing Play-Doh. Why?"

"What else would they do with it?" I asked. "I bet they never use it to make anything."

Just then, Conor started jumping up and down and yelling. I thought maybe Rose and Owen weren't sharing the Play-Doh with him. But what was really happening was that he'd seen something in the trees behind the storage shed in their yard.

"Cat!" he yelled, pointing a finger. "Cat!"

Hannah gasped. "I was right! The gang took Buttercup over there!"

Well, maybe. I thought it was more likely that there was some kind of animal living in the Sunderlands' yard that Buttercup wanted to eat. He didn't seem to be able to stay away from the place. And right then he looked as if he was hunting. He was crouched down with his backside up in the air as he crept slowly forward. When he's like that, it's as if he can't hear or see anything else, he's so determined to get what he's after.

I have nightmares about Buttercup coming for me just like that.

"He's here!" Rose shouted. "Get him, and he's ours!"

The three of them took off like some kind of herd of wild animals. Hannah started after them, but I grabbed her arm.

"Your mother will get mad if we leave the yard again," I reminded her.

"How can we save him from here?" Hannah groaned. "If we only had a helicopter. Or it would be even better if I could fly myself. Then I could just swoop down and get him."

"You'd still have to leave the yard," I pointed out.
"You'd still be in trouble."

"Stop!" Hannah shouted at the Sunderland triplets. "Police! Put your hands up!"

Rose looked over her shoulder at us and laughed.

"We have you surrounded!" Hannah yelled.

The Sunderlands didn't look worried.

They were almost right on top of Buttercup before he noticed them. Then he seemed so startled that he did this leap right into the air and landed on all four feet. He followed that with a little hop.

I wasn't surprised because I saw him turn a somersault once. But Owen went crazy.

"He does tricks!" he screeched.

"Catch him! We can have a circus!"

"We'll be rich!" Rose hollered.

"I wanna cat!" Conor added.

They didn't come close to catching him, of course. Buttercup moved so fast, it was as if he'd been shot out of a cannon. The Sunderlands couldn't keep up.

"Where did he go?" Owen demanded as they ran past us.

"Hey, you can't come over here!" I shouted as I turned and ran after him. "Won't your mother be mad because you left your yard?"

He didn't answer, but I could hear Rose laughing. Then she yelled, "Look in the garage!"

The Dufranes' garage door was wide open because Mrs. D. never shuts it. The Sunderlands went racing in. Hannah stopped at the door and started jumping up and down, trying to reach the handle over her head so she could pull the door down and close it. When that didn't work, she grabbed her bicycle and told me to get her father's.

"We've got to block up this door so they can't get out," she whispered.

I wasn't sure that was a good idea. Why would anyone want to keep the Sunderland triplets in their garage?

"You're under arrest," she told them.

Conor started to cry, then stopped and said, "What?"

"I said you're under arrest," Hannah repeated. "Don't worry. Your parents will be able to visit you."

"You can't arrest us," Rose said.

"Do we get to wear handcuffs?" Owen asked.

"Sorry. I only had one pair, and Hannah broke them," I explained.

"I had to," Hannah said. "You lost the key."

"You can't arrest us, because we didn't do anything," Rose complained.

The real reason we couldn't arrest them was that we weren't really the police.

"You worked with a gang of art thieves so you could steal Buttercup," Hannah explained. "You have to go to jail for that."

"What art thieves? What are you talking about?" Rose asked her.

"The thieves you hired to steal Buttercup," Hannah said.

"We would never hire anyone to steal anything for us," Owen told her. "If we wanted something, we'd just take it ourselves."

"This is stupid. We don't have to stay in here. Come on," Rose snapped at her brothers.

"Stupid, stupid, stupid," Conor sang as he followed his sister.

"I like being in jail," Owen told her. "I want to stay."

"I said *come on,*" Rose repeated.

The three of them pushed their way past the bicycles we'd placed in the opening to the garage. Really, they just walked around them, because two bikes—one of them being a kid's bike—didn't begin to take up enough space to block the whole door.

"Jailbreak!" Hannah shouted.

"Get 'em!" I yelled.

We chased them as far as the woods between the two houses. We had to stop, but they kept going.

"They got away!" I said. "Oh, well. It would have been boring to keep them in the garage very long, anyway."

Hannah started to smile and her eyes got larger. "They've escaped to the badlands! It's a horrible place, really dangerous. It's not safe for normal people. But *they* have their hideout there."

The Sunderland triplets weren't exactly hiding. They'd gone back to throwing Play-Doh. Their lawn, with all the holes they'd dug into it, did look bad, though.

But how long would they stay there?

LOOKING FOR A QUEST

Chapter 8

"I want to go on a quest," Hannah said a couple of days later.

Quests are trips you take to search for something. They're very dangerous. When you're on a quest, you run into things like dragons or sea serpents or wizards.

I love quests.

"We should bring weapons," I suggested. "Or what about a net? We might need to capture someone, and nets are always good for that."

We went up to Hannah's room and found the little backpack she uses when we play mountain climber. Then we went over to her desk where she keeps her old candy from her Christmas stocking and Easter basket. Mostly what she had there was the weird stuff no one wants to eat. The best thing left was an old bunny missing his ears.

"I knew I had some of these," she said as she pulled out a little net bag that still held some chocolate coins wrapped in gold foil. "We'll need this gold if we meet any trolls and have to pay them to let us pass."

"Good idea," I told her.

"I know," she said.

She dropped the candy into her backpack and turned to her toy box. After digging around a bit, she pulled out a jump rope. She rolled it up and forced it down into the pack, too.

I wondered what we were going to do with it, but before I could ask, Hannah was leaving the room.

"Come on," she said. "We need a flashlight."

"But it's not dark yet," I pointed out.

"We may have to go into a dungeon or a cave. We can't play with matches, so we're going to take the big flashlight from the kitchen."

"Oh, that flashlight's really long, too," I reminded Hannah. "We can use it for a sword."

While we were in the kitchen picking up the flashlight, I suggested we throw a box of crackers in the pack, too. And a couple of juice boxes. You never know how long a quest will take.

"Wait just a minute. Where do you guys think you're going?" Mrs. D. asked as Hannah opened the back door.

"On a quest," Hannah answered.

"Not outside you're not. It's raining," Mrs. D. said.

"Don't worry. We'll be safe," I promised.

"And you'll be wet," Mrs. D. objected. "It's been pouring all day."

"You often run into bad weather on quests. Remember when we went on that quest when it was snowing?" Hannah said.

Mrs. D. smiled. "Then put your raincoats on. They're still on the floor in the laundry room where you left them when you came in from school."

"Good," Hannah said as she grabbed hers. "This can be our armor."

My armor is light yellow and has a little extra material on the front of the hood so that I look like a duck. It's bad enough I have to wear the thing to school, but on a quest? And Hannah's armor has a daisy on one of its pink pockets. What dragon or wizard will be afraid of us when we're dressed like that?

"Look for some old boots to put on, too," Mrs. D. ordered. "You should be able to find something in the garage. I don't want you ruining your sneakers."

Like people going on quests worry about their sneakers.

We had our coats on and were going out the door to the garage, when Hannah suddenly stopped and shouted, "Who goes there?"

That is fancy quest talk for *Who's there?* Hannah shouts it a lot when we're on quests. I didn't think anything of it until I looked over her shoulder and saw that someone did "go there."

The Sunderland triplets.

All three of them were in the garage doorway. They were soaking wet because no one makes *them* wear ugly raincoats and boots. It looked as if we'd caught them on their way out because they had their backs to us. Rose turned to look at us for just a second, but Owen and Conor didn't even do that. They just took off when they heard Hannah shout.

And Owen was carrying something.

"The Sunderland triplets just robbed us!" Hannah yelled.

She didn't wait to look for boots. She just started running.

"Get back here!" Mrs. D. called after her from the kitchen door.

Hannah stopped just before she would have started splashing in the puddles in the driveway.

"Why do you think they took something?" her mother asked her.

"Owen was carrying a box," Hannah explained.

"If he was bringing us something, he would have left the box here. Besides," I added, "the Sunderland triplets

don't give things away. They *take* them. You really need to start keeping the garage door closed, Mrs. D."

Mrs. D. sighed and turned back into the kitchen. I followed her and saw her looking out a window that faced the Sunderlands'.

"I think he's got Buttercup's cat carrier," she said. "But he's already in the trees, so I'm not sure. Why would he want that?"

"Where is Buttercup?" Hannah asked from behind me.

"He went outdoors quite a while ago," Mrs. D. answered.

"They've got him then," Hannah said. "They put him in his carrier, and they *stole* him."

"That's right. He scratched Rose when she tried to steal him when we were playing Pinocchio. They took the carrier because they know he won't let people run with him in their arms," I added.

Mrs. D. groaned. "I've already spoken to their mother about them coming over here and chasing Buttercup. It can't be good for him."

I wasn't too worried about Buttercup. Nothing bothered him much. But I did think I could see a good quest coming up.

"Let us leave the yard, and we'll bring him back, Mrs. D.," I offered.

"I could call Mrs. Sunderland again, I suppose," Mrs. D. suggested. "But how do I tell that poor woman that her kids stole our cat carrier and that they may have stolen our cat?"

I was sure she'd heard a lot worse.

"Let us go over there," I said again. "We'll take care of everything."

"Mrs. Sunderland has enough to worry about without you two going over there and accusing her kids of stealing a cat. Go outside and look around for Buttercup in our yard, but you stay away from theirs," Mrs. D. ordered. "We'll find a way to get the cat carrier back later."

Hannah looked at me. Her eyes were big, and she was starting to smile.

"Mrs. Sunderland said Buttercup was dirty, Mom,"

Hannah said as Mrs. D. was on her way out of the room.

Mrs. D. stopped. "What?"

"The first time the Sunderland triplets tried to catch Buttercup, their mother told them he was a dirty stray cat and that they should stay away from him," Hannah said.

Mrs. D. turned around. "She called Buttercup a *stray cat?*"

We both nodded.

"And she said he was nasty and looked as if he had a disease," I added, just in case Mrs. D. needed to hear a little more.

"You guys go over to their yard," she told us. "If they have our cat, you bring him home."

I could tell this was going to be the best quest we'd ever been on.

THE
BEST
QUEST

Chapter 9

"Don't forget the boots!" Mrs. D. insisted as we left the kitchen. So we had to make a stop in the garage to find some old boots that would fit us. By the time we were finally ready to leave, the rain was coming down really hard. You could see great big drops hitting the pavement on the driveway.

Hannah opened her backpack and pulled out the jump rope.

"Grab hold of one end of this," she ordered. "We'll use it to keep us from being separated in the storm."

I started to head outside, but Hannah pulled on the rope and brought me to a halt.

"Hey! I go first," she said.

"Why?"

"Because the person who goes first will be at the front end of the rope and will get to lead the other person," Hannah explained.

"Right. So why do you get to be the leader?"

"Because it's my jump rope. Now come on."

Hannah jerked on the rope and pulled me out into the rain. We didn't waste any time searching her yard. Instead, we rushed across the driveway and then onto the grass, where our boots sank into the wet lawn.

"Quicksand!" Hannah yelled over her shoulder. "Don't panic or you'll sink!"

As if I would panic.

The wind had brought down a long slender branch from one of the trees along the edge of the lawn. I dropped my end of the jump rope just long enough to run over and get it. Then I got back into position, picked up the rope again, and said, "Don't worry, Hannah! We can use this branch to pull ourselves out of the quicksand."

We pretended the branch was lying along the top of wet loose sand that we were stuck in. We pulled ourselves along the stick and were saved.

That's almost always how people on TV get out of quicksand.

One side of the Dufranes' lawn sloped down away from the house. The low spot filled up with water whenever there was a heavy rain, like today.

"We have to find a way to get across this river," Hannah said as she stopped beside the pool that had formed in her backyard. She ran along it, looking for the narrowest spot, pulling me behind her.

Without warning, she jumped over the water. I must have been looking somewhere else, because I didn't see what she was doing. I just felt a big tug on the jump rope. I was pulled right into the water and landed on my knees with a splash.

Hannah turned around. "Hold on to the rope!" she shouted. "I'll pull you out."

She started pulling on the rope so hard and so fast that in order to keep hold of it, I had to wade through the water on my knees. By the time I was able to stand up again, my legs were covered with mud.

That kind of thing happens on quests all the time.

When we got to the row of trees next to the Sunderlands', we stopped.

"We can rest here," Hannah said.

We weren't all that tired, since we'd only run across Hannah's backyard, so we didn't need much of a rest.

"Where do you think they have him?" I asked.

"We can forget about the house because their mother would never let them bring Buttercup in there," Hannah said. "I think we should check that little castle by the edge of the forest. Rose and Conor are headed over there, anyway."

She was talking about the little toolshed at the back of the Sunderlands' yard. Rose and Conor were running toward it.

"Don't let him out yet!" Rose shouted.

Hannah turned to me and whispered, "I told you."

Once Rose and Conor went inside the shed, we crept closer so we could hear what was going on inside.

"Can you believe he went right into this box when we chased him into the garage?" Owen said. He was laughing and squealing. If we could have looked into the shed, I'm sure we would have seen him jumping up and down. "But he's really mad. The whole box was shaking while I was carrying it back. And now look at it! He's hopping around in there like crazy!"

Rose said, "We brought him some bologna. That will fix everything."

Hannah looked at me and made a face. She hates

bologna. Now that she knew they had bologna in there, I guess she decided it was time for us to do something, because she pulled open the shed door and ran in. I got pulled in after her.

"Unhand him!" she yelled.

Unhand him is fancy quest talk like *Who goes there?* It's another thing Hannah likes to shout a lot when we're questing.

"What's she talking about?" Owen asked.

"She wants us to give her the cat," Rose explained. "Forget it. He's ours now because he's on our property." She was standing in front of the box, which was wobbling like mad, as if we were going to have to go through her to get to it. "There's three of us and only two of you. You're not getting our cat."

Rose was right. There *were* three of them. They were younger than I was, but they were Sunderlands. I had Hannah on my side, of course, but that made things even worse. I knew she would fight to the death.

I'm not really into fighting to the death.

Then I saw Hannah drop her rope and reach into her backpack. She pulled out the gold coins and spread them across her hand so everyone could see them.

"Gold," she said.

The Sunderlands didn't seem too interested.

"*Candy,*" I told them.

Hannah threw the coins into a corner of the shed behind a broken sled.

Conor shrieked and went running after them. We could hear him behind us, crying and throwing things around as he hunted for Hannah's old chocolate.

Now there were only two of them. That was still too many Sunderlands.

I took a step forward and in a very serious voice said, "Remember, we're older and bigger than you guys are. We don't want to hurt you. We just want the cat. Give him to us, and we'll leave you alone."

Rose laughed, and Owen threw himself down on

top of the cat carrier. That helped to keep it from bopping all over the place, but it meant we'd have to pull him away before we could get to Buttercup.

The situation looked pretty hopeless.

Then I heard a humming noise behind me. When I looked over my shoulder, I saw that Hannah had the flashlight in one of her hands. She had turned it on and was holding it upright in front of her while she made a whirring noise.

"What is she doing?" Owen asked, standing up so he could see what was going on.

"Oh, no! She's turned on the atomic sword!" I cried. "Run! Save yourselves while you can!"

None of the Sunderlands moved an inch. Conor was still in the corner, licking chocolate off the gold wrapper of one of the candy coins. Rose and Owen just stood there staring at Hannah. She started waving the flashlight back and forth, lunging at them, and making this low noise as if a motor was running in the flashlight.

"What is that thing?" Owen asked.

"It's just a flashlight," Rose told him. But her head started weaving back and forth as she followed the light Hannah was waving madly in front of her.

I could see that Hannah was trying to force them back. If they moved, she'd be able to grab the cat carrier. Which meant that she would get to fight off the Sunderland triplets with the atomic sword *and* save Buttercup.

Well, she was just going to have to share.

While Rose and Owen were distracted, I gave them both a shove, reached between them for the cat carrier, and ran out into the yard.

I could tell Hannah was right behind me, because she was yelling, "Give it to me, Brandon! It's my cat carrier!"

I could feel Buttercup throwing himself around inside the carrier, trying to get away. And that was *before* I had to start jumping over the holes Owen had dug all over the lawn. I ran and jumped holes. Buttercup bumped up and down in his box.

Conor howled, "Cat! Cat!"

Rose and Owen yelled, "Stop him!"

And Hannah shouted, "Brandon! You're ruining everything! Give Buttercup to me!"

I didn't think everything was ruined. I kind of liked the way things were turning out.

We came to a particularly big hole filled with rainwater. I ran around it to the right, and Hannah ran around it to the left. We nearly crashed into each other when we reached the other side.

She grabbed my arm, the one that was holding Buttercup's box, and pulled it toward her. I pulled back.

"Give it to me, Brandon!"

"They're going to catch us! Let me go!"

"It's my cat!"

"I'm company!"

Rose and Owen splashed through the hole behind us. They were just reaching their arms out to push and grab when we all saw something moving out of the woods behind the yard.

We stopped short and watched Buttercup make his

way across a corner of the Sunderlands' lawn toward Hannah's. He didn't look as if he cared at all that we were on a quest to save him.

As I watched him, I could still feel something jumping around inside the carrier Hannah and I were struggling over.

"You can have it," I said to her.

She screamed and threw the box as far away from us as she could. It landed on the ground with a bounce, and when it landed again, the door popped open.

Something long and red flew out of it. It stopped on the lawn as if it was confused.

"Stupid Owen!" Rose yelled. "You caught a squirrel."

"Squirrel!" Conor shrieked. "Wanna squirrel!"

"What's going on? What's going on?" Mrs. Sunderland hollered from the back of the house.

"We've got a squirrel, Mom!" Owen shouted. "Can we keep it?"

"Oh, no! Oh, no!" Mrs. Sunderland cried as she

ran out into the rain. "Squirrels have diseases! Leave it alone!"

The squirrel saw all the Sunderlands coming toward him. He pulled himself together and ran for the trees.

So did we. Hannah stopped just long enough to grab Buttercup's cat carrier, and then we were off.

We could hear Conor carrying on about how he wanted a squirrel. Owen insisted that Rose had made him catch it. Rose said she did not. And Mrs. Sunderland told them all to stay away from squirrels because they weren't much better than rats with bushy tails.

We crossed the river and quicksand a lot faster on our way back across the yard, especially since we'd left the jump rope in the shed.

When we got to the back of Hannah's house, we found Buttercup lying on the floor of the garage, out of the rain.

"Oh, Buttercup! You are saved!" Hannah exclaimed. She knelt down beside him and dragged him into her arms.

He yawned.

"How can he be saved when he was never in danger?" I asked.

"The Sunderlands came over here to get him, so he was in danger."

"He saved himself, then. He always does. The next time he's in danger, I'm staying here and watching TV."

Hannah started to smile. "The next time, he'll be in danger because he's a prince trapped in a cat's body by an evil wizard."

I hate princes. They almost always have to marry somebody.

"I want to be the evil wizard," I said.

That is a part I would love.